A Jar of Tiny Stars

Poems by
NCTE Award-Winning Poets

Bernice E. Cullinan, *Editor*

Illustrations by Andi MacLeod

Portraits by Marc Nadel

WORDSONG • *BOYDS MILLS PRESS*
NATIONAL COUNCIL OF TEACHERS OF ENGLISH

Published by Wordsong
Boyds Mills Press, Inc.
A Highlights Company
815 Church Street
Honesdale, Pennsylvania 18431
Printed in Mexico

Publisher Cataloging-in-Publication Data
Main entry under title.
        A jar of tiny stars : poems by NCTE award-winning poets / Bernice E. Cullinan,
editor ; illustrations by Andi MacLeod ; portraits by Marc Nadel. — 1st ed.
[96]p. : ill. , ports. ; cm.
Bibliography.
Includes index.
Summary : A sample of poems by poets who have received the National Council of Teachers
of English Award for Poetry for Children, including David McCord, Aileen Fisher, Karla
Kuskin, Myra Cohn Livingston, Eve Merriam, John Ciardi, Lilian Moore, Arnold Adoff,
Valerie Worth, and Barbara Esbensen.
ISBN 1-56397-087-2
NCTE Stock Number: 25069-3050
1. Children's poetry, American. [1. American poetry — Collections.]
I. Cullinan, Bernice E., editor. II. MacLeod, Andi, ill. III. Nadel, Marc, ill. IV. Title.
811.54 — dc20   1995
Library of Congress Catalog Card Number 93-60466   CIP

First edition, 1996
Book designed by Charlotte Staub
The text of this book is set in Cochin.
The illustrations are done in pen and ink; the portraits are done in watercolor washes.

10 9 8 7 6 5 4 3 2

ACKNOWLEDGMENTS

A special thanks goes to the following teachers:

Lucille Allaire, Clover Street School
Kay Allison, Barbour Elementary School
Carla Avery, Fairglen Elementary School
Gwen Barrett, Russel School
Beth Beach, John Harshaw School
Karen Beard, Vineyards Elementary School
Bev Blumberg, Loomis School
Ruth Bowers, Fairglen Elementary School
Sue Bradin, Fairglen Elementary School
Kristin Braig, Rose Tree Elementary School
Elaine Braus, Springdale School
K. Buckshaw, Holbrook School
Diana Burger, Wetherill School
Phoebe Cascaden, Delcroft Elementary School
Patricia Ciotoli, Glenwood Elementary School
Ruth Gail Cohen, Worrall School
Ed Conti, Guggenheim School
Charlene Cox, Lakeview School
Donna Crasky, Rose Tree Elementary School
Kelly Crooks, Woodlyn School
Martha Dachos, Wallingford Elementary School
Christine Dano, Rose Tree Elementary School
Jim DeRose, Wallingford Elementary School
Lynne Dewees, Indian Lane Elementary School
Helene Dichter, Worrall School
Lisa Dowd, Worrall School
Patricia Downes, Mile Creek School
K. Driscoll, Luxmanor Elementary School
Mary Anne H. Dugan, Pennell Elementary School
Gayle Durrance, Vineyards Elementary School
Kathleen Edwards, Vineyards Elementary School
Sandy Eshleman, Coeburn Elementary School
Gail Falkoff, P.S. 79 Queens
Mary Falls, Park Lane Elementary School
Carol Flamini, Culbertson Elementary School
Susan Fournier, Main Street School
Rosemary Fowler, Coeburn Elementary School
Heather Garbarino, Tioga Elementary School
Mary S. Gaynor, Ivy Drive School
Anthony Gervase, Barbour Elementary School
Bobbie Gettis, Pennell Elementary School
Heather Giancola, Springdale School
Diane Ginn, Columbus School
Shirley Graham, Latimer Lane School
Debbie Greene, Winship School
Rhonda Greer, Vineyards Elementary School
Andrea Gresko, Donnelly Elementary School
Rebecca Griffing
    Harry L. Johnson Elementary School
Heidi Gross, Havertown, PA
Peggy Harrison, Wickliffe School
Laura Heald, Vineyards Elementary School

Dorrie Hess, Latimer Lane School
Laura Hietpas, Fairglen Elementary School
Kathleen Holder, John Harshaw School
Carolyn Hollaway, Vineyards Elementary School
Kathy Irons, Sharon Hill Elementary School
David Johnson, Robert Sanders School
Lisa Johnson, Holly Oak School
Joyce A. Joyce, Pennell Elementary School
Louise A. Kanaley, French Road Elementary School
Jane Kershner, Park Lane Elementary School
Sharon Ketts, Archer Community School
Angela King, Vineyards Elementary School
Lynn Klempner, Russell School
Judith Kolbenschlag, Harry L. Johnson School
Ethel Kozak, Fairglen Elementary School
Terrie Lang, Fairglen Elementary School
Mattie Lewis, Wallingford Elementary School
Joanne Payne-Lionetti, Marion Street School
Rosina Lizzul, P.S. 130 Brooklyn
Mary Lou Lohr, Walnut Street Elementary School
Cathy Cummings Lyttle, Adamsville School
Lois Makucin, Clover Street School
Betty J. Maness, Toby Farms Elementary School
Miriam Marecek, Early Childhood Education
    Boston University
Marianne Marino, Central School
Sandra Markon, The Rashi School
Renee Martin, Media, PA
Judy Matsko, Amoslana School
Angela Matt, Loomis School
Veronica McDermott, Patchogue-Medford Schools
Jane McDevitt, Russell School
Linda McKinley, Fairglen Elementary School
Terrie Mitev, Vineyards Elementary School
Mary Ellen Moyher, Springdale School
Ellen M. Mullins, Green Ridge Elementary School
Ellie Murray, Culbertson Elementary School
Helen Naab, Loomis Elementary School
Jean Nash, Claude Chester Elementary School
Sherry Nash, Russell School
Kathy Navarre, Pennell Elementary School
Kathleen Nevins, Concord Elementary School
Mimi Olsen, Guggenheim School
Cheryl Papa, Hillcrest School
Maryann M. Parker, Whitney Point Middle School
Joan Pearlman, The Pingry School
Pat Pendergast, Worrall School
Deborah G. Pot, Pennell Elementary School
Mona Potter, Priscilla Purse, Wayne, PA
    Fairglen Elementary School
Linda Ratta, Claude Chester School
Peg Reed, Wickliffe School

Deborah Revels, Fairglen Elementary School
Nancy Rogalsky, Farm Hill School
Linda Rohlfs, Martin School
Molly Rosenberg, Pennell Elementary School
Toni Sandlin, Culbertson Elementary School
Maureen Sato, Holly Oak School
Millie Seeds, Culbertson Elementary School
Katherine Shuter, Concord Elementary School
Mary Small, Worrall School
Dr. Nick Spennato, Media, PA
Susan Soxman, Worrall School
Elena Starr, Concord Elementary
John Steczak, Rose Tree Elementary School
Rhoda J. Steiger, Stillmeadow School
Ann Stevenson, Green Ridge Elementary School
Linda Stickney, Vineyards Elementary School
Cheryl Stroud, Community School District Two
Sherry Tavegie, Meadow Lark Grade School
Jennie Teti, Russell School

Laurie Thomas, Guggenheim School
Wanda Thomas, Highland Park School
Nancee Beidler-Torns, Anna Reynolds School
Patricia Towne, Parkside Elementary School
Maureen Tracy, Parkside Elementary School
Barbara Tucker, Springdale School
Phyllis E. Tyler,
   Walnut Street Elementary School
Margaret Wales, Pennell Elementary School
Marilyn Walsh, Agassiz School
Marie Wardynski, Delcroft Elementary School
Chris Weil, Locust Valley Intermediate
Renee Weinstein, Loomis Elementary School
Patricia Wolff, P.S. 41 Manhattan
Patricia Woody, John Harshaw School
Deborah Wooten, P.S. 126 Manhattan;
Anne Wuthrich, Vineyards Elementary School
Joanne Zeccarelli,
   Vineyards Elementary School

And thanks also to Valerie Hess, Hofstra University, and Ann Lovett, Manhasset, for tabulating children's responses.

The title for this book was taken from Lilian Moore's poem "If You Catch a Firefly."

CONTENTS

Dedicated to Jonathan Paul Cullinan
(1969 - 1975),
a boy who loved poetry

The National Council of Teachers of English
Award for Poetry for Children is presented once every three
years to a poet for a distinguished body of work sustained
over a period of time and honors the memory of
Jonathan Paul Cullinan,
a child who loved books.

INTRODUCTION

The ten poets featured here received an important award: The National Council of Teachers of English Award for Excellence in Poetry for Children. The award, given to poets judged to be the *very best,* is for the entire body of their work, not for just a single book or poem. From 1977 to 1982, the award was given once each year; since then it is given every three years. This book celebrates the award winners.

How were the poems selected? Teachers and librarians across the United States tried out a sampling of each poet's work to see which poems children liked best. More than 3,500 kids read and listened to the poems—then ranked their top five choices for each poet. The national field test showed that children like poems they can understand: ones that make them laugh and ones that tell a story. The poems that children like best by the award-winning poets appear in this book.

Bernice E. Cullinan
Professor, New York University
and Editor-in-Chief, Wordsong

David McCord

"One of my teachers told me, 'Never let a day go by without looking on three beautiful things.' I try to live up to that and find it isn't difficult. The sky in all weathers is, for me, the first of these three things."

— David McCord

Every time I climb a tree
Every time I climb a tree
Every time I climb a tree
I scrape a leg
Or skin a knee
And every time I climb a tree
I find some ants
Or dodge a bee
And get the ants
All over me

And every time I climb a tree
Where have you been?
They say to me
But don't they know that I am free
Every time I climb a tree?
I like it best
To spot a nest
That has an egg
or maybe three

And then I skin
The other leg
But every time I climb a tree
I see a lot of things to see
Swallows rooftops and TV
And all the fields and farms there be
Every time I climb a tree
Though climbing may be good for ants
It isn't awfully good for pants
But still it's pretty good for me
Every time I climb a tree

The pickety fence
The pickety fence
Give it a lick it's
The pickety fence
Give it a lick it's
A clickety fence
Give it a lick it's
A lickety fence
Give it a lick
Give it a lick
Give it a lick
With a rickety stick
Pickety
Pickety
Pickety
Pick

SNOWMAN

My little snowman has a mouth,
So he is always smiling south.
My little snowman has a nose;
I couldn't seem to give him toes,
I couldn't seem to make his ears.
He shed a lot of frozen tears
Before I gave him any eyes —
But they are big ones for his size.

THE STAR IN THE PAIL

I took the pail for water when the sun was high
And left it in the shadow of the barn nearby.

When evening slippered over like the moth's brown wing,
I went to fetch the water from the cool wellspring.

The night was clear and warm and wide, and I alone
Was walking by the light of stars as thickly sown

As wheat across the prairie, or the first fall flakes,
Or spray upon the lawn—the kind the sprinkler makes.

But every star was far away as far can be,
With all the starry silence sliding over me.

And every time I stopped I set the pail down slow,
For when I stooped to pick the handle up to go

Of all the stars in heaven there was one to spare,
And he silvered in the water and I left him there.

I HAVE A BOOK

that has no cover
where there used to be a lady
and her knighted lover.
Oh, her lover was a knight
and his armor fitted right.
While he hadn't any horse,
still I always thought he might;
and I always thought of course
he'd be riding far away,
for the day was good and bright
though the tree was big and shady.
Now there isn't any lady
and there isn't any knight,
and there never was a horse,
so there never was a fight.
And the book all by itself
is sort of lonely on the shelf.

Aileen Fisher

"When I was young there was still quite a bit of logging nearby, and my brother and I used to follow the iced logging roads. . . . [now] I live in Boulder, Colorado, at the edge of town on a dead-end street, close to Flagstaff Mountain. The highlight of each day is a walk with my dog and a friend and her dog on one of the many trails nearby. This keeps me in touch with the weather, the wildlife, and the wonderful scenery in every direction."

—Aileen Fisher

MY PUPPY

I have a playful
prankish pup:

When I stoop down
he prances up

And snuffs my neck
and slicks my ear

As if I'd been
away a *year*:

I say, "Be good,
you prankish pup."

But he just smiles
and eats me up!

MY CAT AND I

When I flop down
to take a rest
my cat jumps up
upon my chest.

She kneads my sweater
with her paws . . .
and sometimes even
uses claws.

She rubs my chin
and purrs away,
as if I am
a game to play!

CRICKET JACKETS

The day a cricket's jacket
gets pinchy, he can crack it
and hang it on a bracket
as he goes hopping by.

He doesn't need a mother
to go and buy another,
he doesn't need a mother,
and I will tell you why:

Beneath the pinchy jacket
the cricket sheds with vigor
he has a new one growing
that's just a little bigger,
to last him till July.

And then, again, he'll crack it,
his pinchy cricket jacket,
and hang it on a bracket
as he goes hopping by.

OUT IN THE DARK
AND DAYLIGHT

Out in the dark and daylight,
under a cloud or tree,

Out in the park and play light,
out where the wind blows free,

Out in the March or May light
with shadows and stars to see,

Out in the dark and daylight . . .
that's where I like to be.

LISTEN, RABBIT!

I saw him first
when the sun went down
in the summer sky
at the edge of town
where grass grew green
and the path grew brown.

I couldn't tell
what he was at all
when I saw him first,
sort of halfway small,
sort of halfway grown,
near a gray old stone
in the field, alone.

Then I saw his ears
standing rabbit tall!

I stood as still
as a maple tree
and I looked at him
and he looked at me . . .
with only one eye
that I could see,
bulging out
on the side of his head.

"Nice little rabbit,"
I softly said
inside myself,
though I hoped he'd hear
with two long ears
standing up so near
and my thoughts so clear.

My heart went thump!
And do you know why?
'Cause I hoped that maybe
as time went by
the rabbit and I
(if he felt like *me*)
could have each other
for company.

Note: This is only part of "Listen, Rabbit!" Read the entire poem in Aileen Fisher's book *Listen, Rabbit!*

Karla Kuskin

"If there were a recipe for a poem, these would be the ingredients: word sounds, rhythm, description, feeling, memory, rhyme and imagination. They can be put together a thousand different ways, a thousand, thousand . . . more."

—Karla Kuskin

HUGHBERT AND THE GLUE

Hughbert had a jar of glue.
From Hugh the glue could not be parted,
At least could not be parted far,
For Hugh was glued to Hughbert's jar.
But that is where it all had started.
The glue upon the shoe of Hugh
Attached him to the floor.
The glue on Hughbert's gluey hand
Was fastened to the door,
While two of Hughbert's relatives
Were glued against each other.
His mother, I believe, was one.
The other was his brother.
The dog and cat stood quite nearby.
They could not move from there.
The bird was glued securely
Into Hughbert's mother's hair.

Hughbert's father hurried home
And loudly said to Hugh:
"From now on I would rather
That you did not play with glue."

18

THE MEAL

Timothy Tompkins had turnips and tea.
The turnips were tiny.
He ate at least three.
And then, for dessert,
He had onions and ice.
He liked that so much
That he ordered it twice.
He had two cups of ketchup,
A prune, and a pickle.
"Delicious," said Timothy.
"Well worth a nickel."
He folded his napkin
And hastened to add,
"It's one of the loveliest breakfasts I've had."

19

I WOKE UP THIS MORNING

I woke up this morning
At quarter past seven.
I kicked up the covers
And stuck out my toe.

And ever since then
(That's a quarter past seven)
They haven't said anything
Other than "no."

They haven't said anything
Other than "Please, dear,
Don't do what you're doing,"
Or "Lower your voice."

Whatever I've done
And however I've chosen,
I've done the wrong thing
And I've made the wrong choice.

I didn't wash well
And I didn't say thank you.
I didn't shake hands
And I didn't say please.

I didn't say sorry
When passing the candy
I banged the box into
Miss Witelson's knees.
I didn't say sorry.
I didn't stand straighter.
I didn't speak louder
When asked what I'd said.

Well, I said
That tomorrow
At quarter past seven
They can
Come in and get me.
I'm Staying In Bed.

WINTER CLOTHES

Under my hood I have a hat
And under that
My hair is flat.
Under my coat
My sweater's blue.
My sweater's red.
I'm wearing two.
My muffler muffles to my chin
And round my neck
And then tucks in.
My gloves were knitted
By my aunts.
I've mittens too
And pants
And pants
And boots
And shoes
With socks inside.
The boots are rubber, red and wide.
And when I walk
I must not fall
Because I can't get up at all.

LEWIS HAS A TRUMPET

A trumpet
A trumpet
Lewis has a trumpet
A bright one that's yellow
A loud proud horn.
He blows it in the evening
When the moon is newly rising
He blows it when it's raining
In the cold and misty morn
It honks and it whistles
It roars like a lion
It rumbles like a lion
With a wheezy huffing hum
His parents say it's awful
Oh really simply awful
But
Lewis says he loves it
It's such a handsome trumpet
And when he's through with trumpets
He's going to buy a drum.

Myra Cohn Livingston

"When I watched my young daughter trying to learn how to roller-skate, I wrote '74th Street.' 'Hey, this little kid gets roller skates. / She puts them on. / She stands up and almost / flops over backwards. . . . '

"My daughter starting, then falling, then starting again with many kinds of movements inspired a different sort of poem. . . . The words, the sound of them, needed to fit the content of what they said."

—Myra Cohn Livingston

KITTENS

Our cat had kittens
weeks ago
when everything outside was snow.

So she stayed in
and kept them warm
and safe from all the clouds and storm.

But yesterday
when there was sun
she snuzzled on the smallest one

and turned it over
from beneath
and took its fur between her teeth

and carried it
outside to see
how nice a winter day can be

and then our dog
decided he
would help her take the other three

and one by one
they took them out
to see what sun is all about

so when they're grown
they'll always know
to never be afraid of snow.

LEMONADE STAND

Every summer
under the shade
we fix up a stand
to sell lemonade.

A stack of cups,
a pitcher of ice,
a shirtboard sign
to tell the price.

A dime for the big,
A nickel for small.
The nickel cup's short.
The dime cup's tall.

Plenty of sugar
to make it sweet,
and sometimes cookies
for us to eat.

But when the sun
moves into the shade
it gets too hot
to sell lemonade.

Nobody stops
so we put things away
and drink what's left
and start to play.

ARTHUR THINKS ON KENNEDY

When Kennedy
Come to our town
He come with dreams
Got shot right down.

It rained all morning.
You can bet
They didn't want him
Getting wet.

They put a bubble
On his car
So we could see him
From afar.

But then the sun
Come out, so they
Just took the bubble
Clean away.

When Kennedy
Come to our town
Some low-down white folks
Shot him down,

And I got bubbles,
I got dreams,
So I know what
That killing means.

SHELL

When it was time
for Show and Tell,
Adam brought a big pink shell.

He told about
the ocean roar
and walking on the sandy shore.

And then he passed
the shell around.
We listened to the water sound.

And that's the first time
I could hear
the wild waves calling to my ear.

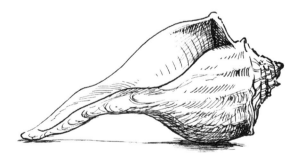

MARTIN LUTHER KING

Got me a special place
For Martin Luther King.
His picture on the wall
Makes me sing.

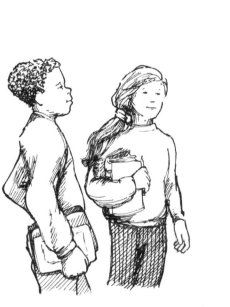

I look at it for a long time
And think of some
Real good ways
We will overcome.

Eve Merriam

"I've sometimes spent weeks looking for precisely the right word.
It's like having a tiny marble in
your pocket, you can just feel it.
Sometimes you find a word and
say, 'No, I don't think this is it. . . .'
Then you discard it, and take
another and another until you get
it right. I do think poetry is great
fun. That's what I'd like to stress
more than anything else: the joy
of the sounds of language."

— Eve Merriam

Gooseberry
Juice berry,
Loose berry jam.

Spread it on crackers,
Spread it on bread,
Try not to spread it
Onto your head.

Gooseberry,
Juice berry,
Loose berry jam.

No matter how neatly
You try to bite in,
It runs like a river
Down to your chin.

Gooseberry,
Juice berry,
Loose berry jam.

HOW TO EAT A POEM

Don't be polite.
Bite in.
Pick it up with your fingers and lick the juice that
      may run down your chin.
It is ready and ripe now, whenever you are.

You do not need a knife or fork or spoon
      or plate or napkin or tablecloth.

For there is no core
or stem
or rind
or pit
or seed
or skin
to throw away.

SKIP ROPE RHYME FOR OUR TIME

Junk mail, junk mail,
look look look:
bargain offer coupon,
catalogue book.

Junk mail, junk mail,
free free free:
trial sample,
guarantee.

Here's an offer
you can't let pass:
an artificial lawn
with real crab grass.

Twenty cents off,
just go to the store
and buy what you don't want,
then buy some more.

Junk mail, junk mail,
what's my name?
My name is Dear Occupant
and yours is the same.

WINDSHIELD WIPER

fog smog	fog smog
tissue paper	tissue paper
clear the blear	clear the smear
fog more	fog more
splat splat	downpour
rubber scraper	rubber scraper
overshoes	macintosh
bumbershoot	muddle on
slosh through	slosh through
drying up	drying up
sky lighter	sky lighter
nearly clear	nearly clear

clearing clearing veer
clear here clear

UMBILICAL

You can take away my mother,
you can take away my sister,
but don't take away
my little transistor.

I can do without sunshine,
I can do without Spring,
but I can't do without
my ear to that thing.

I can live without water,
in a hole in the ground,
but I can't live without
that sound that sound that sound that sOWnd.

John Ciardi

"Poetry and learning are both fun, and children are full of an enormous relish for both. My poetry is just a bubbling up of a natural foolishness, and the idea that maybe you can make language dance a bit."

—John Ciardi

MUMMY SLEPT LATE AND DADDY FIXED BREAKFAST

Daddy fixed the breakfast.
He made us each a waffle.
It looked like gravel pudding.
It tasted something awful.

"Ha, ha," he said, "I'll try again.
This time I'll get it right."
But what *I* got was in between
Bituminous and anthracite.

"A little too well done? Oh well,
I'll have to start all over."
That time what landed on my plate
Looked like a manhole cover.

I tried to cut it with a fork:
The fork gave off a spark.
I tried a knife and twisted it
Into a question mark.

I tried it with a hack-saw.
I tried it with a torch.
It didn't even make a dent.
It didn't even scorch.

The next time Dad gets breakfast
When Mommy's sleeping late,
I think I'll skip the waffles.
I'd sooner eat the plate!

WHAT DID YOU LEARN
AT THE ZOO

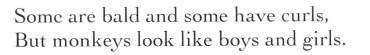

What did I learn at the zoo?
Monkeys look like you.

Some are bald and some have curls,
But monkeys look like boys and girls.

Some are quiet and some make noise,
But all of them look like girls and boys.

What did *you* learn at the zoo?
Oh, much the same as you:

Gorillas are good, gorillas are bad,
But all of them look a lot like Dad.

Some do one thing, some another,
But all of them scream a lot like Mother.

What did *we* learn at the zoo?
Just what we wanted to:

That it's fun to tease if you make it rhyme
(Though you mustn't do it all the time),
That kangaroos hop and monkeys climb,
And that a bottle of lemon-and-lime
Is a very good way to spend a dime.

(And so is a bag of peanuts.)

THE HAPPY FAMILY

Before the children say goodnight,
    Mother, Father, stop and think:
Have you screwed their heads on tight?
    Have you washed their ears with ink?

Have you said and done and thought
    All that earnest parents should?
Have you beat them as you ought?
    Have you begged them to be good?

And above all—when you start
    Out the door and douse the light—
Think, be certain, search your heart:
    Have you screwed their heads on tight?

If they sneeze when they're asleep,
    Will their little heads come off?
If they just breathe very deep?
    If—especially—they cough?

Should—alas!—the little dears
    Lose a little head or two,
Have you inked their little ears:
    Girls' ears pink and boys' ears blue?

Children's heads are very loose.
     Mother, Father, screw them tight.
If you feel uncertain use
     A monkey wrench, but do it right.

If a head should come unscrewed
     You will know that you have failed.
Doubtful cases should be glued.
     Stubborn cases should be nailed.

Then when all your darlings go
     Sweetly screaming off to bed,
Mother, Father, you may know
     Angels guard each little head.

Come the morning you will find
     One by one each little head
Full of gentle thoughts and kind,
     Sweetly screaming to be fed.

SOMETIMES *I FEEL THIS WAY*

I have one head that wants to be good,
     And one that wants to be bad.
And always, as soon as I get up,
     One of my heads is sad.

"Be bad," says one head. "Don't you know
     It's fun to be bad. Be as bad as you like.
Put sand in your brother's shoe—that's fun.
     Put gum on the seat of your sister's bike."

"What fun is that?" says my other head.
     "Why not go down before the rest
And set things out for breakfast? My,
     That would please Mother. Be good—that's best."

"What! Better than putting frogs in the sink?
     Or salt in the tea-pot? Have some fun.
Be bad, be bad, be good and bad.
     You know it is good to be bad," says One.

"Is it good to make Sister and Brother sad?
     And Mother and Daddy? And when you do,
Is it good to get spanked? Is it good to cry?
     No, no. Be good—that's best," says Two.

So one by one they say what they say,
    And what they say is "Be Good—Be Bad."
And if One is happy that makes Two cry.
    And if Two is happy that makes One sad.

Someday maybe, when I grow up,
    I shall wake and find I have just one—
The happy head. But which will it be?
    I wish I knew. They are both *some* fun.

SUMMER SONG

By the sand between my toes,
By the waves behind my ears,
By the sunburn on my nose,
By the little salty tears
That make rainbows in the sun
When I squeeze my eyes and run,
By the way the seagulls screech,
Guess where I am? *At the* . . . . . !
By the way the children shout
Guess what happened? *School is* . . . . . !
By the way I sing this song
Guess if summer lasts too long:
You must answer Right or . . . . . !

Lilian Moore

"Poetry should be like fireworks, packed carefully and artfully, ready to explode with unpredictable effects. When people asked Robert Frost—as they did by the hundreds—what he meant by 'But I have promises to keep / And miles to go before I sleep / And miles to go before I sleep,' he always turned the question aside with a joke. Maybe he couldn't answer it, and maybe he was glad that the lines exploded in so many different colors in so many people's minds."

—Lilian Moore

IF YOU CATCH A FIREFLY

If you catch a firefly
    and keep it in a jar
You may find that
    you have lost
A tiny star.

If you let it go then,
    back into the night,
You may see it
    once again
Star bright.

I LEFT MY HEAD

I left my head
somewhere
today.
Put it down for
just
a minute.
Under the
table?
On a chair?
Wish I were
able
to say
where.
Everything I need
is
in it!

MINE

I made a sand castle.
In rolled the sea.
      "All sand castles
      belong to me —
      to me,"
said the sea.

I dug sand tunnels.
In flowed the sea.
      "All sand tunnels
      belong to me —
      to me,"
said the sea.

I saw my sand pail floating free.
I ran and snatched it from the sea.
      "My sand pail
      belongs to me —
      to ME!"

RECESS

The children
scribble their shadows
on the school yard,

scribble
scribble
on a great blackboard—

lanky leg
shadows
running into
lifted arm shadows
flinging
bouncing ball shapes
into skinny upside down shadows
swinging
on
long monkey bars

till
a cloud
moving
across the morning sun
wipes out all
scribbles
like a giant
eraser.

CONSTRUCTION

The giant mouth
chews
rocks
spews them
and is back for
more.

The giant arm
swings up
with a girder
for
the fourteenth floor.

Down there,
a tiny man
is
telling them
where
to put a skyscraper.

51

Arnold Adoff

"Most of the time, almost all of the time, I want my poems to do more than prose can do. So if I want to just say, 'Dear Mom, I am fine at camp,' I don't have to write a poem. But if I'm going to be a poet, if I'm poeting, if I'm writing poems, I want to do more in my poems than just present facts or feelings or communicate. I want my poems to sing as well as to say."

—Arnold Adoff

FLAVORS

Mama is chocolate: you must be swirls
of dark fudge,
and ripples
through
your cocoa
curls;

chips
and
flips of sprinkles
on your
summer
face.

FLAVORS

Daddy is vanilla: you must be mean
old
bean
in the morning,
cherry
chunks by afternoon,
and
sweet
peach sometimes.

But mostly   you
are vanilla
up
your
arms.

FLAVORS

Me
is better
   butter: I must be
            pecans
                  roasted,
                  toasted;

almond
wal nut   three
        scoop combination
               cone:
melting under
        kisses.

It is a new color.
It is a new flavor.
      For
        love.

Coach Says: Listen Sonny, You Are The Safety On This Team, And Your Body Belongs To Me, And Your Safety Is The Last Thing On Your Mind. Right? Right. Their Guy Is Super Fast. Do Not Let Him Get Past. Period. Understood? Safety Last. Now Play It By The Numbers.

Simple.

    We start with eleven   when the whistle blows,

    and

        their quarterback   throws his pass.

                Simple.

Number One: He throws the ball.

Number Two: The ball is caught.

Number Three: Their receiver runs

                d o w n   the field

                  toward me.

Number Four

Through Ten: My team

        mates   who ought to stop him   are hit

    or

    fall, or miss, or are too slow to make

                the play.

Simple.

    Safety last. I am the last of our eleven,

        and the runner   runs my way.

BLACK IS BROWN IS TAN

black   is brown   is tan
is girl   is boy
is nose   is face
is all the colors
of the race

is dark   is light
singing songs
in singing night
kiss big woman   hug big man
black   is brown   is tan

this is the way it is for us   this is the way we are

Note: This is only part of "black is brown is tan." Read the entire poem in Arnold Adoff's book *black is brown is tan.*

57

Valerie Worth

". . . Never forget that the subject is as important as your feeling: The mud puddle itself is as important as your pleasure in looking at it or splashing through it. Never let the mud puddle get lost in the poetry — because, in many ways, the mud puddle *is* the poetry."

— Valerie Worth

dinosaurs

Dinosaurs
Do not count,
Because
They are all
Dead:

None of us
Saw them, dogs
Do not even
Know that
They were there —

But they
Still walk
About heavily
In everybody's
Head.

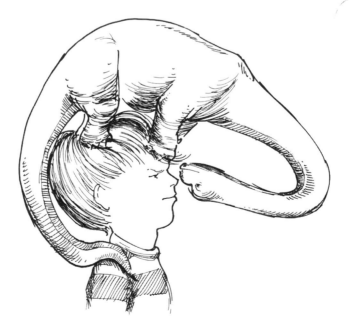

lawnmower

The lawnmower
Grinds its teeth
Over the grass,
Spitting out a thick
Green spray;

Its head is too full
Of iron and oil
To know
What it throws
Away:

The lawn's whole
Crop of chopped
Soft,
Delicious
Green hay.

giraffe

How lucky
To live
So high
Above
The body,
Breathing
At heaven's
Level,
Looking
Sun
In the eye;
While down
Below
The neck's
Precarious
Stair,
Back, belly,
And legs
Take care
Of themselves,
Hardly
Aware
Of the head's
Airy
Affairs.

safety pin

Closed, it sleeps
On its side
Quietly,
The silver
Image
Of some
Small fish;

Opened, it snaps
Its tail out
Like a thin
Shrimp, and looks
At the sharp
Point with a
Surprised eye.

pebbles

Pebbles belong to no one
Until you pick them up—
Then they are yours.

But which, of all the world's
Mountains of little broken stones,
Will you choose to keep?

The smooth black, the white,
The rough gray with sparks
Shining in its cracks?

Somewhere the best pebble must
Lie hidden, meant for you
If you can find it.

Barbara Esbensen

"I think about the images first and the rhyme only incidentally. With rhyme you always have a sense of what's coming at the end of the line, and that ruins the surprise. To me, poetry should knock your block off."

—Barbara Esbensen

BAT

Every night
a short word
covered with fur   mouth open
flies
out of dark libraries

All day it hangs
upside-down in the card
catalog   under B

But at sundown   B A T
by the hundreds
leaves the gloomy
pages
of mystery books   crawls
out of damp bindings
and   g l i d e s   into the night air
shaking itself free
of the trailing old words
DRACULA   BLOOD   FANG. . .

ELEPHANT

The word is too heavy
to lift   too cumbersome to
lead through a room filled with
relatives or small
glass trinkets

ELEPHANT

He must have invented it
himself. This is a lumbering
gray word   the ears of it
are huge and flap like loose
wings   a word with
wrinkled knees and toes
like boxing gloves

This word   E L E P H A N T
sways toward us   bulk
and skull-bones filling up
the space   trumpeting
its own wide name
through its nose!

MY CAT

My cat is asleep—white paws
folded under
his chin   He is a soft gray
smudge on the round rug

Dozing in the sun
He is a warm round stone
with a fur collar

My cat is taking
a nap   Not a whisker
trembles   Not a hair
moves   His breath goes
softly in and out

Stay in your holes
mice!   My cat sees you
in his dreams
and he has left
his motor running!

PENCILS

The rooms in a pencil
are narrow
but elephants   castles and
watermelons
fit in

In a pencil
noisy words yell for attention
and quiet words wait their turn

How did they slip
into such a tight place?
Who
gives them their
lunch?

From a broken pencil
an unbroken poem will come!
There is a long story living
in the shortest pencil

Every word in your
pencil
is fearless   ready to walk
the blue tightrope lines
Ready
to teeter and smile
down   Ready to come right out
and show you
thinking!

SNAKE

The word begins to
hiss as soon as the first
letter
goes on   S
s-s-s-s-s-s   forked tongue flickers
Hard eyes stare

Already the rest of the poem
shrinks back from
his narrow speed   The paper
draws in its breath   S N A K E
loops around the pencil
slides
among typewriter keys   slips
like a silk shoelace
away

About the Poets

David McCord

"I seemed to know instinctively that to write for the young I had to write for myself. I write out of myself, about things I did as a boy, about things that are fairly timeless as subjects. . . .

"Children love words, rhythm, rhyme, music, games. They climb trees, skate, swim, swing, fish, explore, act, ride, run, and love snow and getting wet all over; they make things and are curious about science. They love humor and nonsense and imaginary conversations with imaginary things; they are closer to the sixth sense than we who are older." [1]

You May Want to Know

David McCord worked at Harvard University for thirty-seven years serving as fund-raiser, alumni editor, and historian but, all the while, he continued to write poetry for children. He is the author or editor of fifty books of poetry, essays, history, medicine, light verse, and verse for children. He is also an artist and has had several one-man shows of watercolor landscapes. He lives at the Harvard Club and is an avid fan of the Boston Red Sox.

David McCord was awarded the first honorary degree of doctor of humane letters ever granted at Harvard; it was conferred on him at the same ceremonies at which President John F. Kennedy received an LL.D.

In 1983, Simmons College in Boston, Massachusetts, presented him with a doctor of children's literature degree. The citation states:

". . . as a poet who has dedicated your life to the creation of poetry which opens the ears of children to the nuances of language and to the splendors of the world which language represents, you have spoken in a unique voice. You have brought to bear upon your work your long and thorough investigation of and fascination with the natural world, the social world, the world of the intellect, and the world of the imagination.

. . . You have helped awaken adults to the sounds of the child's world. . . . The poet John Ciardi has said, 'One is too few of [you] and there is, alas, no second.'" In 1977 he was the first recipient of the NCTE Award for Excellence in Poetry for Children.

David McCord was born on November 15, 1897, near Greenwich Village, New York City. He grew up on Long Island, in Princeton, New Jersey, and on a ranch by the Rogue River in Oregon.

Aileen Fisher

"I try to be at my desk four hours a day, from eight A.M. to noon. Ideas come to me out of experiences and from reading and remembering. I usually do a first draft by hand. I can't imagine writing verse on a typewriter, and for years I wrote nothing but verse so I formed the habit of thinking with a pencil or pen in hand. I usually rework my material, sometimes more, sometimes less. I never try out my ideas on children, except on the child I used to know—me! Fortunately, I remember pretty well what I used to like to read, think about, and do. I find even today that if I write something I like, children are pretty apt to like it, too. I guess what it amounts to is I never grew up." [2]

You May Want to Know

Aileen Fisher likes to work with wood she finds in the forest; she doesn't change its shape but looks for shapes that are already in the wood, then she polishes the wood and mounts it to bring out its own tendencies. This is similar to the way she works with words when she writes poetry; she searches for just the right word and then polishes it to bring out the spirit of the poem.[3]

Aileen Fisher was born September 9, 1906, in Iron River, Michigan. She attended the University of Chicago and received her bachelor of journalism from the University of Missouri. She worked at the Women's Journalistic Register and the Labor Bureau of the Middle West before she devoted herself to writing full time.

She received the NCTE Award for Excellence in Poetry for Children in 1978.

Karla Kuskin

"Poetry is a *required* taste. There are many children's books in my workroom. When my daughter Julia was ten she was thumbing through them in search of treasure. 'What's this one?' she asked, holding it up. 'That's verse,' I said. 'Yum,' said Jool, disappearing into a book. For Julia poetry is delicious, a *required* taste like milk and cookies. I couldn't agree with her more.

"Instead of building a fence of formality around poetry, I want to emphasize its accessibility, the sound, rhythm, humor, the inherent simplicity. Poetry can be as natural and effective a form of self-expression as singing or shouting." [4]

You May Want to Know

Karla Kuskin is an artist as well as a poet; she illustrates most of the books she writes. She designed the medallion for the NCTE Poetry Award; when she won it three years later (1979), her friends teased her, "Will you create other awards that you might win?"

Karla's student project became her first book, *Roar and More*. She created it in a graphics art course while working on her master's degree at the Yale School of Design.

Karla Kuskin was born on July 19, 1932, in New York City. She lives in Brooklyn, New York, and continues to write poetry for children.

Myra Cohn Livingston

"In my creative-writing workshops and classes for young people, kindergarten through twelfth grade, and in my teaching at college level, I encourage students to approach their own writing and sharing of poetry with attention to established tradition and craft where needed, but to seek innovative patterns and language where they seem essential. It is in this way, I believe, that all of us grow." [5]

"What definition is there to encompass all the poems that have meaning and appeal to children? Do not definitions belong, rather, to science, to the laboratory? Our varying emotions, our needs as human beings, are not so easily stuffed into formulas and test tubes. The language of experience, of feeling, is not . . . the language of classification, and the point of poetry is not to arrive at a definition but to arrive at an experience—to feel, to bring our emotions and sensitivities into play." [6]

You May Want to Know

Myra Cohn Livingston was born on August 17, 1926, in Omaha, Nebraska. She began writing poetry at age five; she later wrote plays and showed talent for music and sculpture. Myra's family moved from Omaha to Los Angeles when she was eleven years old; there she worked on the school newspaper. After graduating from Sarah Lawrence College, Myra returned to California and now lives in Beverly Hills.

She received the NCTE Award for Excellence in Poetry for Children in 1980.

Eve Merriam

"You may not 'get' all of a poem the first time you read it, because the words and the built-in music are so concentrated. Don't let it worry you; just go on to the end and then go back and read it again. You will find that the meaning begins to shine through. For a poem, with its rhythmic effects and use of word-pictures, has more than one level to explore. It becomes like a stone that you skim onto a lake; the ripples widen. New meanings unfold, and you have the pleasure of discovering more and more each time." [7]

You May Want to Know

Eve Merriam was born in Philadelphia and graduated from the University of Pennsylvania. She did graduate work at the University of Wisconsin and Columbia University. After graduation from college, Eve worked as a sales clerk in a department store and as a fashion copywriter at *Glamour* magazine. She was also a playwright; several of her plays have been produced as Broadway and off-Broadway musicals. Eve lived in Greenwich Village, New York City, because she loved the rhythms and sounds of the city.

Eve won the NCTE Award for Excellence in Poetry for Children in 1981. She died in 1992.

John Ciardi

"I dislike most of the children's poems I see because they seem written by a sponge dipped in warm milk and sprinkled with sugar. Children, as I know them from my own childhood and from my present parenthood, run to violent emotions. One of the best things children's poetry can do is to catch up that violence in the measure and play of rhyme, rhythm, and form—and so make a pleasant, if momentary, assurance of it." [8]

"Teachers can't say, 'Memorize . . . and give it back on demand. . . .' They are the ones who must entice the student. If a student can be brought to say 'Wow!' to one poem, he or she can say 'Wow!' to another. . . . Unless we lead students to this contact, Pac-Man is going to eat us all." [9]

You May Want to Know

John Ciardi (1916 - 1986) taught at the University of Kansas City, Harvard University, and Rutgers University. He served as director of the Bread Loaf Writers' Conference at Middlebury College, received international acclaim for his translation of Dante's *Inferno*, served as poetry editor of *Saturday Review* (1956 - 1972), served as host of the CBS show *Accent,* and wrote the definitive textbook on poetry, *How Does a Poem Mean?* (1959). He received the Prix de Rome from the American Academy of Arts and Letters in 1956 and the NCTE Award for Excellence in Poetry for Children in 1982.

John Ciardi, the only son of Italian immigrants, graduated magna cum laude from Tufts University in 1938 and received his M.A. in English literature from the University of Michigan the following year. Although he died in 1986, he lives on in the hearts of children because of the delight in language he shared with them through his poetry.

Lilian Moore

"When you hear a poem that sounds exactly right—when the words and the feelings seem inevitably to belong together—it is easy to believe that the poem, particularly if it is a poem for children—sprang full blown from the brow of the poet.

"Most of the poets I know work hard. The grain of sand that's supposed to irritate the creative center and produce a pearl often produces just the irritation. Lines that are supposed to dance sometimes drag their iambic feet. Words that were supposed to reflect light remain maddeningly dim. Or a cliché pops up that must be uprooted like a noxious weed. Then it's back to the typewriter, or the ball-point pen, or the pencil with a good eraser. And another wastebasket to fill." [10]

You May Want to Know

Lilian Moore was born in New York City. She attended New York City schools, Hunter College, and did graduate work at Columbia University. She taught school in New York City and worked in a publishing house. She now lives on a farm in upstate New York.

In 1985 she received the NCTE Award for Excellence in Poetry for Children.

Arnold Adoff

"Every day I go into my room and write. My wife, Virginia Hamilton, and I work each morning from about 7 A.M. to 1 P.M. in separate rooms. Sometimes I write on yellow paper, writing and rewriting lots of drafts. A group of students who visited me at home called me 'the popcorn poet' because I fill my wastebasket with balls of crumpled up paper—drafts I reject." [11]

"In the past ten years I have made a concentrated effort to create a body of work: a family of young voices, through collections of my own poetry, that speak to, and through, the times of youth. My young people play sports and eat flying oatmeal cookies and search for interracial identities, and care about a solid hug." [12]

You May Want to Know

Arnold Adoff has a love affair with food. Since he works at home he is able to cook at the same time he is composing poems; he sometimes pauses from his work to stir the soup or punch down the bread dough. His passion for food is evident in his collections of poems *Eats*, *Greens*, and *Chocolate Dreams*. Once he was eating peanut butter while he was typing. He got peanut butter in the typewriter, and a repairman had to come and fix it.

Arnold Adoff was born July 15, 1915, in the East Bronx section of New York City. He received his B.A. from City College and attended Columbia University and the New School for Social Research. He was a teacher in the New York Public Schools in Harlem and the Upper West Side. He has taught at New York University and Connecticut College. He and his wife, author Virginia Hamilton, live in Yellow Springs, Ohio. Their two grown children, Leigh and Jamie, are both involved in the world of music.

He won the NCTE Award for Excellence in Poetry for Children in 1988.

Valerie Worth

"I write about what is vivid, exciting, magical to me—about the way I see things now, or how I viewed them as a child—or a combination of both child/adult feelings. I write about things that strike a chord in me, be it a lawnmower or a kaleidoscope or coat hangers. I have strong responses to what finds its way into my work.

"I would say write poetry for the fun of it, for the joy of it, for the love of it. And especially for the love of the things you write about, whatever they may be—whether beautiful or ugly, grand or humble, birds of paradise or mosquitoes, stars or mud puddles: All are worthy of being written about if you feel a deep affection for them—or, indeed, if you feel strongly about them in any way at all.

"It has always seemed to me that any tree or flower, any living creature, even any old board or brick or bottle possesses a mysterious poetry of its own, a poetry still wordless, formless, inaudible, but asking to be translated into words and images and sounds—to be expressed as a poem. . . . Poetry is simply a way of revealing and celebrating the essentially poetic nature of the world itself." [13]

You May Want to Know

Valerie Worth was born October 29, 1933, in Philadelphia, Pennsylvania. Her father taught biology at Swarthmore College and joined The Rockefeller Foundation as a field biologist to study typhus. The family traveled to Bangalore, India, so her father could study malaria. Valerie attended one year of high school in Bangalore but later returned to Swarthmore for her bachelor of arts in English.

She received the NCTE Award for Excellence in Poetry for Children in 1991. She died in 1994.

Barbara Esbensen

"As a child growing up in Madison, Wisconsin, I read everything in sight, and drew pictures on anything that looked like it needed decoration. I wrote stories with my two best friends, and we all intended to be writers. We decided that I could always illustrate their books, in case my own efforts at writing didn't get me anywhere.

"When I was 14-and-a-half and in the 10th grade, my English teacher, Eulalie Beffel, looked at a poem I had written, and told me I was 'a writer.' When she introduced me to poets like Amy Lowell, Stephen Vincent Benét and Emily Dickinson, she literally changed my life. Until then, I had not known that it was possible to use words in such exciting ways." [14]

"No matter what form my writing takes, I have tried to be as accurate with images of the natural world when I write poetry as I have had to be when writing books about the loon, the great horned owl, or the otter."

You May Want to Know

Barbara Esbensen was born in Madison, Wisconsin in 1925 and spent the first twenty years of her life there. She graduated from the University of Wisconsin, majoring in Art Education. After receiving her degree, she taught art and creative writing to young adults on the tropical island of Truk in the Eastern Caroline Islands. Later, she taught third grade in Eureka, California.

Barbara Esbensen and her husband, Tory, have had six children, Julie, Peter, Daniel, Jane, George, and Kai. Peter died when he was nineteen. All of the others are grown now. She says, "We live in Edina, Minnesota where I write in a lovely (but not orderly) tree-high room with big windows on three sides, and a sassy squirrel just outside the bay. Sometimes all three cats are draped over the furniture up there."

She received the NCTE Award for excellence in Poetry for Children in 1994.

1. Hopkins, Lee Bennett, *Pass the Poetry, Please!* (New York: HarperCollins, 1987), p. 107.
2. Hopkins, Lee Bennett, "Profile: Aileen Fisher," *Language Arts* (October 1978), Vol. 55, pp. 869, 871.
3. Fisher, Aileen, Promotional Material, Thomas Y. Crowell, 1978.
4. Kuskin, Karla, Promotional Material, HarperCollins, 1979.
5. Livingston, Myra Cohn, Promotional Material, McElderry Books, 1990.
6. Livingston, Myra Cohn, *Climb into the Bell Tower* (HarperCollins, 1990), p. 23.
7. Merriam, Eve, *What Can a Poem Do? An Explanation for Children and for Those Who Work with Children* (Atheneum, 1962), pp. 1-4.
8. Ciardi, John, *Something about the Author: Autobiography Series* (Detroit, MI: Gale Research), p. 61.
9. Hopkins, Lee Bennett, *Pass the Poetry, Please!* (New York: HarperCollins, 1987), p. 13.
10. Koenig, Rachel, *Something about the Author*, Vol. 52 (Detroit, MI: Gale Research), p. 129.
11. Adoff, Arnold, "Interview with Arnold Adoff," Promotional Material, Harcourt Brace, 1988.
12. Adoff, Arnold, "Politics, Poetry, and Teaching Children: A Personal Journey," *The Lion and the Unicorn*, 1986, Vol. 10, p. 9.
13. Hopkins, Lee Bennett, "Profile: Valerie Worth," *Language Arts*, (October 1991), Vol. 68, pp. 499-500.
14. Harper Collins Promotional Material

BIBLIOGRAPHY

*This bibliography is intended as a resource
for further reading and highlights certain works by the poets.
Some books are omitted due to space limitations.*

David McCord

All Small: Poems by David McCord. Illus. Madelaine Gill Linden. Little Brown, 1986.

Away and Ago: Rhymes of the Never Was and Always Is. Illus. Leslie Morrill. Little Brown, 1975.

Every Time I Climb a Tree. Illus. Marc Simont. Little Brown, 1967.

One at a Time. Illus. Henry B. Kane. Little Brown, 1986.

The Star in the Pail. Illus. Marc Simont. Little Brown, 1975.

Aileen Fisher

Always Wondering: Some Favorite Poems of Aileen Fisher. Illus. Joan Sandin. HarperCollins, 1991.

Anybody Home? Illus. Susan Bonners. HarperCollins, 1980.

The House of a Mouse. Illus. Joan Sandin. HarperCollins, 1988.

Like Nothing at All. Illus. Leonard Weisgard. HarperCollins, 1979.

Listen, Rabbit! Illus. Symeon Shimin. HarperCollins, 1964.

Out in the Dark and Daylight. Illus. Gail Owens. HarperCollins, 1980.

Rabbits, Rabbits. Illus. Gail Niemann. HarperCollins, 1983.

When It Comes to Bugs. Illus. Chris and Bruce Degen. HarperCollins, 1986.

Karla Kuskin

Any Me I Want to Be. HarperCollins, 1972.

Dogs and Dragons, Trees and Dreams: A Collection of Poems. HarperCollins, 1980.

Herbert Hated Being Small. Houghton Mifflin, 1979.

Near the Window Tree: Poems & Notes. HarperCollins, 1975.

Myra Cohn Livingston

Birthday Poems. Illus. Margot Tomes. Holiday House, 1989.

Celebrations. Illus. Leonard Everett Fisher. Holiday House, 1985.

Earth Songs. Illus. Leonard Everett Fisher. Holiday House, 1986.

Higgledy-Piggledy: Verses and Pictures. Illus. Peter Sis. McElderry Books, 1986.

I Like You, If You Like Me: Poems of Friendship. McElderry Books, 1987.

Space Songs. Illus. Leonard Everett Fisher. Holiday House, 1988.

There Was a Place and Other Poems. McElderry Books, 1988.

Up in the Air. Illus. Leonard Everett Fisher. Holiday House, 1989.

Eve Merriam

Blackberry Ink. Illus. Hans Wilhelm. Morrow, 1985.

Chortles: New and Selected Wordplay Poems. Illus. Sheila Hamanaka. Morrow, 1989.

Fresh Paint. Illus. David Frampton. Macmillan, 1986.

It Doesn't Always Have to Rhyme. Atheneum, 1964.

Jamboree: Rhymes for All Times. Illus. Walter Gaffney-Kessell. Dell, 1984.

Poem for a Pickle: Funnybone Verses. Illus. Sheila Hamanaka. Morrow, 1989.

You Be Good and I'll Be Night: Jump on the-Bed Poems. Illus. Karen Lee Schmidt. Morrow, 1988.

John Ciardi

Doodlesoup. Illus. Merle Nacht. Houghton Mifflin, 1985.

I Met a Man. Illus. Robert Osborn. Houghton Mifflin, 1961.

The Man Who Sang the Sillies. Illus. Edward Gorey. HarperCollins, 1981.

The Monster Den: or Look What Happened at My House—and to It. Illus. Edward Gorey. Wordsong/Boyds Mills Press, 1991.

The Reason for the Pelican. Illus. Dominic Catalano. Wordsong/Boyds Mills Press, 1994.

Someone Could Win a Polar Bear. Illus. Edward Gorey. Wordsong/Boyds Mills Press, 1993.

You Know Who. Illus. Edward Gorey. Wordsong/Boyds Mills Press, 1991.

You Read to Me, I'll Read to You. Illus. Edward Gorey. HarperCollins, 1962.

Lilian Moore

I Feel the Same Way. Illus. Robert Quackenbush. Macmillan, 1976.
Something New Begins. Illus. Mary J. Dunton. Macmillan, 1982.
Think of Shadows. Illus. Deborah Robison. Atheneum, 1980.

Arnold Adoff

All the Colors of the Race. Illus. John Steptoe. Lothrop, 1982.
Chocolate Dreams. Illus. Turi MacCombie. Lothrop, 1989.
Eats. Illus. Susan Russo. Lothrop, 1979.
Friend Dog. Illus. Troy Howell. HarperCollins, 1980.
Hard to Be Six. Illus. Cheryl Hanna. Lothrop, 1991.
In for Winter, Out for Spring. Illus. Jerry Pinkney. Harcourt Brace, 1991.
Sports Pages. Illus. Steve Kuzma. HarperCollins, 1986.

Valerie Worth

All the Small Poems. Illus. Natalie Babbitt. Farrar Straus Giroux, 1987.
More Small Poems. Illus. Natalie Babbitt. Farrar Straus Giroux, 1976.
Small Poems. Illus. Natalie Babbitt. Farrar Straus Giroux 1972.
Small Poems Again. Illus. Natalie Babbitt. Farrar Straus Giroux, 1985.
Still More Small Poems. Illus. Natalie Babbitt. Farrar Straus Giroux, 1978.

Barbara Esbensen

Cold Stars and Fireflies: Poems of the Four Seasons. HarperCollins, 1984.
Ladder to the Sky: A Retelling of an Ojibway Legend. Little, Brown, 1989.
The Star Maiden: A Retelling of an Ojibway Legend. Little, Brown, 1988.
Who Shrank My Grandmother's House? Poems of Discovery. HarperCollins, 1992.
Words with Wrinkled Knees: Animal Poems. HarperCollins, 1986.

PERMISSIONS

Every possible effort has been made to trace the ownership of each poem included in *A Jar of Tiny Stars*. If any errors or omissions have occurred, corrections will be made in subsequent printings, provided the publisher is notified of their existence.

Permission to reprint copyrighted poems is gratefully acknowledged to the following:

Myra Ciardi for "Summer Song" and "The Happy Family" from *The Man Who Sang the Sillies* by John Ciardi. Copyright © 1961 by John Ciardi; "Mummy Slept Late and Daddy Fixed Breakfast," "Sometimes I Feel This Way," and "What Did You Learn at the Zoo?" from *You Read to Me, I'll Read to You* by John Ciardi, published by J. B. Lippincott Company, 1962, and Harper Trophy Books, 1987. Reprinted with permission.

Farrar, Straus & Giroux Inc. for "Dinosaurs," "Lawnmower," "Giraffe," "Safety Pin," and "Pebbles" from *All the Small Poems* by Valerie Worth. Copyright © 1987 by Valerie Worth. Reprinted by permission of Farrar, Straus & Giroux Inc.

Aileen Fisher for "Out in the Dark and Daylight," "My Puppy," "My Cat and I," and "Cricket Jackets" from *Out In the Dark and Daylight* by Aileen Fisher. Copyright © 1980 by Aileen Fisher; and text excerpt "I saw him first...could have each other for company" from *Listen, Rabbit* by Aileen Fisher. Copyright © 1964 by Aileen Fisher. Reprinted by permission of the author.

HarperCollins Publishers for "Lewis Has a Trumpet," "The Meal," "Hughbert and the Glue," and "I Woke Up This Morning" from *Dogs & Dragons, Trees & Dreams* by Karla Kuskin. Copyright © 1980 by Karla Kuskin; and for "Bat," "Elephant," and "Snake" from *Words with Wrinkled Knees* by Barbara Juster Esbensen. Copyright © 1986 by Barbara Juster Esbensen; "My Cat" and "Pencils" from *Who Shrank My Grandmother's House? Poems of Discovery* by Barbara Juster Esbensen. Copyright © 1992 by Barbara Juster Esbensen; "Coach Says Listen Sonny" from *Sports Pages* by Arnold Adoff. Copyright © 1986 by Arnold Adoff. Reprinted by permission of HarperCollins Publishers.

Karla Kuskin for "Winter Clothes" from *The Rose on My Cake* by Karla Kuskin, published by Harper & Row. Copyright © 1964 by Karla Kuskin. Reprinted by permission of the author.

Lothrop, Lee & Shepard Books for "Mama is Chocolate," "Daddy is Vanilla," and "Me is Better Butter" from *All the Colors of the Race* by Arnold Adoff. Copyright © 1982 by Arnold Adoff. Reprinted by permission of Lothrop, Lee & Shepard Books, a division of William Morrow & Co., Inc.

David McCord for "Every time I Climb a Tree," "The Pickety Fence," "Snowman," "The Star in the Pail," and "I have a Book" from *One At a Time* by David McCord. Copyright © 1977 by David McCord. Reprinted by permission of the author.

Margaret K. McElderry Books for "Kittens," "Lemonade Stand," and "Shell" from *Worlds I Know and Other Poems* by Myra Cohn Livingston. Copyright © 1985 by Myra Cohn Livingston. Reprinted by permission of Margaret K. McElderry Books, an imprint of Simon & Schuster Children's Publishing Division.

Marian Reiner for "Arthur Thinks on Kennedy" and "Martin Luther King" from *No Way of Knowing Dallas Poems* by Myra Cohn Livingston. Copyright © 1980 by Myra Cohn Livingston; "I Left My Head," "Mine," and "Recess" from *Something New Begins* by Lilian Moore. Copyright © 1967, 1969, 1972, 1975, 1980, 1982 by Lilian Moore; "If You Catch a Firefly" from *I Feel the Same*

INDEX

by AUTHOR, *Title*, and First Line

93